UNEXPECTED PERFORMANCE

UNEXPECTED PERFORMANCE

Robert Sneed

Published 2014 by Shorehouse Books
Printed in the United States of America

ISBN 0-615-97310-8
EAN-13 978-061597310-4

This book is dedicated to all free spirits who dance to the rhythm of life.

ACKNOWLEDGMENTS

First of all I have to thank my co-worker, friend, mentor, and published author Deb Martin-Webster for opening my eyes to the possibilities of becoming a writer. Thank you for your insight into this new expression of me.

Second I must thank my co-worker Linda, aka Lily, in Unexpected Performance. She came up with the idea of creating a Segway ballet after we both saw a gentleman come into the museum on a Segway PT unit.

I would be remiss if I did not thank the original Magnificent Seven Audio Team – Deb, Peg, Linda, Bridget, Diana, Terry, and Robert. Your daily humor always keeps me laughing.

A special thank you goes to all of the hosts at BH, who stand post on a daily basis. This inspired me to include standing post in the story of Gunter the Frugal Mouse.

A great big thank you goes to Deb, Pete, and Ellen for reading my manuscript, pointing out my spelling and grammar errors, as well as suggestions for the preparation of the manuscript for publication and book cover.

To the memory of KBW my spiritual mentor whose life altering teachings guide me daily.

To the memory of Thomas, my wonderful Siamese cat, who is named Swanson in Unexpected Performance. He was a magnificent being who did sit on the toilet seat for our morning talks. He also sat up like a dog for his treats, and did head rolls down the sidewalk during our leased walks. It is an honor to salute his memory and the wonderful times we had together.

To my friend Bill Andersen who has taught me the difference between mind full and mindful. Thank you for this valuable insight and lesson.

This manuscript would never have been published without the guidance of Donna, Ed, and staff at HO Press and Shorehouse Books. Thank you so much for putting up with this "newbie" and bringing this story into creation.

Table of Contents

Swanson and DJ Begin the Day

Why is it, when you get to the most exciting part of your dream, the alarm clock buzzes? Murphy's Law . . . No! I set the alarm. Apologies Murphy, you scapegoat idol. It is now 5:30 AM, and I must convince my mind, body, and spirit to think about moving. After all, I do have to be at work by 7:30. But my dream! It was so nice, so peaceful, so calm, and so uneventful. But it did have potential to become something unique and wonderful. Maybe it's a blessing that one never, or sometimes never, completes their dream. That way you can create any ending you wish and be completely satisfied for the rest of the day.

It's time for the getting up game. Swanson, my six year old male Siamese cat, who rules this house, helps me play the game. After much face patting, purring, and nose rubbing, Swanson lets out a few loud meows, and the game begins. Throw the left leg out, swing the right leg over, and push up to a sitting position. Bend forward to retrieve glasses from the night stand. Put them on. Take a deep breath and slide off the bed into a standing position. "What do you think about that?" Swanson. A few loud meows confirm my progress. Swanson then heads toward the kitchen for his food and personal hygiene. Taking care of him, I head to the bathroom to take care of my personal hygiene. While brushing my teeth, Swanson came in to sit on top of the closed toilet seat to have our morning conversation. I have no idea what we talk about, but it is always intense. I shave with an electric razor. While that is buzzing, Swanson sits on the toilet seat with his eyes closed contemplating his next subject of discourse. As soon as the razor stops, the conversation begins again. We have much fun and solve many problems.

Oh, before I forget. My name is Daniel Jeremiah Cuddles. Friends call me either D.J., or Cuddles. Either one is fine with me. I work in a museum, out from town, on the lovely estate of the late Beatrice and George Benburger of Benburger Boeuf Burger International. It is said that eating one of George's boeuf burgers is a gastronomic delight! I totally agree. Only the best grade of beef and spices are used to create a juicy, thick burger that melts in your mouth.

In my department, Guest Services, we wear a special uniform. Black sox first, followed by whatever colored underwear you prefer, including a T shirt. Black trousers follow. Since I am built like Sponge Bob Square Pants, I have to use a pair of black designer suspenders to hold them up. A white shirt is next, sporting a paisley tie of a red, black, and silver design, smartly hidden under a black vest. Black shoes complete the lower ensemble. A black blazer, black top coat, and black hat complete the total outfit. "OK," Swanson. "This penguin is ready for the day. Give me a high five, and I'm on my way." Swanson slaps my outstretched palm and utters a few meows. "Hey," buddy. "This afternoon we will leash up and go for a walk. You can do your head rolls down the sidewalk." I do not know where Swanson learned to do this, but it is his favorite performance pastime while walking.   He also sits up like a dog for his treats. Swanson is such an amazing cat, and he knows it!

After a quick stop at Mickey D's for a sausage egg McMuffin and senior coffee with two creams, this Penguin headed out to join the traffic for a dare devil race to Benburger Estate.   The traffic light seemed red forever! The same news repeated itself constantly on the car radio, to the point that I could repeat it verbatim. The green arrow finally popped into view, and I turned left onto the estate road. Stopping at the security gate to swipe my entrance badge, I greeted the security guards. Letting out a sigh, I took a deep breath and settled down to drive the two plus miles to the employee parking lot.

A calm feeling always presents itself when I drive onto the estate. It is out of the loop of busy city traffic, with people rushing to get to their next destination. Driving to the parking lot always gives me the opportunity to view the land and to look for new changes taking place with Mother Nature's gift of constant beauty, no matter what the season.

Being too early for a shuttle, I enjoyed the walk from the parking lot to the museum. It was a sunny, fall day in early November. The sound of my footsteps echoed through the still morning mingled with the sound of birds and wild turkeys. One never knew just when the turkeys might jump onto the roadway and walk in front of you. After all, they do own the estate! There are deer and bear on the estate as well, and I have seen them at a distance. I always walk on the main road.   I don't need to encounter a mother bear and her cubs along a wooded walking trail. As I continued my walk, I noticed how the lush evergreen trees of pine, fir, hemlock, spruce, and holly offered a sharp contrast to the naked dogwood, redbud, maple, and birch trees. Distant sounds of gas driven leaf blowers and trucks ushered in the day.

Turning the corner onto the approach road, Benburger Manor came into view. The house is situated on three thousand acres surrounded by beautiful English formal gardens, a pond, and lush forests. The exterior of the house is embellished with Tennessee Marble, a type of crystalline limestone found primarily in the eastern part of Tennessee. Its pinkish gray color enhances the lovely green boxwoods outlining the house. The formal entrance is enclosed by a large archway supported by massive square stone columns. Several turrets with peaked roofs accent the architecture. A round bay window to the left of the front door accommodates the grand staircase leading up to the second and third floors.

Going into the museum, a small ticket counter is situated to the right of the front door for visitor information and ticket purchases. All rooms on the first and second floors have fireplaces, now fitted with gas logs. Central heating warms the entire house.

On the right side of the entrance hall, the first room that comes into view is the formal dining room. For breakfast and lunch, a small dining room is located next to the formal dining room. A morning room continues from the small dining room and is used for intimate family gatherings and informal entertaining. The kitchen, butler's pantry, and storage rooms are located on the north side of the house underneath the turret section.

The first room to the left of the entrance hall is the formal sitting room, often called the parlor. Next to the parlor is the library. A large music room is located at the far end of the entrance hall. The grand staircase, leading up to the second and third floors, presents a vision of beauty, flooded with light from the huge three story bay window. Stairs across from the grand staircase, on the first floor, lead down to the lower level of the house.

Storage rooms, a wine cellar, and a laundry room are located on the lower level. A game room features a table for American pocket billiards and one for French billiards, called Carom. Playing games of chess and dominos are also available in this room. A gym with weights and other exercise equipment completes the down stairs living space. A second set of stairs leads from the lower level to the kitchen area along the north turret wall, and continues up to the third floor, mainly for servants' use.

On the second floor, the master bedroom suite is located across the front of the house. Additional bedrooms and a large guest parlor complete the second floor. The servants' quarters are located on the third floor with their own parlor. Bathrooms are located throughout the entire house, although none are for public use. Restrooms, the Tack Room Gift Shop, and the Horseshoe Cafe are located a short distance from the house in the horse stable, newly renovated to accommodate visitor's needs.

As I walked down the approach road, the early morning sunlight accentuated the glow of the Tennessee marble, and the museum seemed to come alive with the expectation of a glorious day. The grounds crew was busy cleaning up any trash that littered the approach road, especially in front of the house. It was Christmas at the museum, and time to plan the Hanging of the Greens ceremony. The cold wind hurried my steps inside to begin the day.

Good Morning, Benburger Museum

The museum was bustling with activity. A hardy "good morning" to the security guard led me down some steps into the break room. There, I grabbed that last cup of coffee to fortify me for the day's adventures that lay ahead. Finishing my coffee, checking my schedule, and clocking in, I climbed the stairs to the main floor.

The floral staff was pushing carts of flowers checking old floral arrangements that needed to be refreshed. Hosts were checking each room to see that all antique treasures were accounted for. The workday was upon us!

I work in the audio department at the museum. The audio offers visitors a look into the life of the Benburgers. After all, this was their home. The program gives visitors the opportunity to meet the family and to learn of Mr. Benburger's business empire. The daily routine of the family members and servants offers stories, special events, and funny mishaps that personalize their everyday life. Antique furniture and paintings are detailed, including past history, and their essential value to the museum today.

Simone, Vera, Agnes, Maggie, Seth, Lily, and DJ, known as the Magnificent Seven Audio Team, begin the day wrapping audios. Wrapping is the process of inserting a headset into each audio. The audios are then placed on pegs on a wooden cart that holds 210 audios.

Two carts have to be wrapped before 9 AM, the time the house opens, to be distributed to visitors who have purchased audio tour tickets.   Morning conversations are always interesting.   The more talk, the faster the wrapping.

"Did anyone watch the Zombie movie on TV last night?" asked Simone.

"I prefer the vampire series myself," Seth added.

"I don't like that type of show," said Lily. "I watched Sound of Music. It was lovely."

"What is the house count today?" asked Agnes.

"Beat's me. I forgot to look at the computer in the break room. Does anyone know the count?" asked D.J.

"I think it's around 2500," said Maggie.

"Did you hear about Mary Ellen? She fell and broke her hip," exclaimed Vera. "She is an accident waiting to happen. I told her not to go skiing, but she never listens to anyone."

"We should send her a get well card. Is she in the hospital? I must call Sue to find out. Bless her heart," said Lily.

"Who is the host in charge today?" asked D.J.

"I think its Alice," said Simone.

"She is so nice to work with," added Lily.

"Did anyone get today's rotation schedule?" inquired Seth. "I can't remember if I'm an A or a C. I hate the C schedule. You have to work in the entrance hall all day with lunch at 2:00. That's not right. My stomach demands a 12 noon lunch time."

"That's nothing!" exclaimed Agnes. "I closed audio three days in a row. I keep emailing management about changing my schedule, but they never seem to get the message. I have meetings to go to and doctor appointments to keep. No one seems to care, except me."

"You would have better luck if you just told the host in charge to mark the changes in the schedule book early enough for them to call another replacement host," added Maggie.

"It's 8:42. Better finish that second cart. Do you need help?" asked Simone.

"No, we are almost finished," confirmed Lily.

"Alice is coming down the hall with our rotation schedules," said Vera.

"Are there any audio tours today?" questioned D.J.

"Yes," said Alice. "We have a group of 57 at 9:30 and another group of 35 at 2:00. So look sharp and be ready."

"Did anyone bring the radios up from the break room?" asked Seth.

"I did," replied Simone. "They are in the audio room."

"So, who goes up to the entrance hall, and who stays back here to continue wrapping?" continued Seth.

"Agnes and Lily go up to D, Simone goes to FC, D.J. goes to I rotation, Vera goes to EH, and Seth and Maggie continue wrapping," said D.J., reading a schedule and then handing one to each audio host.

"Every one better check their e-mail before leaving," Agnes suggested.

"Good idea," agreed Seth.

So, what does an A going to I and a C going to D mean? The audio host schedule is divided into the number of hosts available per day, with a regular listing of A through G. An H and I rotation are added on busy days for reserve audio hosts. Because the house opens at 9:00 AM and closes at 4:30 PM, different rotations are assigned every half - hour for the day. These rotations are also given a letter. D stands for the distribution of audios. Visitor instruction is designated with the letter I. EH stands for entrance hall audio host. W stands for wrapping, and FC stands for the front counter audio cart. So, if you are an A, you follow the A schedule including the half-hour rotations assigned to that schedule. Today is Tour Bus Tuesday. Heads up!

Oh yes, do you remember Agnes telling everyone to "check their email" before beginning the day? The audio team has a special phrase to announce that one is going to the rest room. We are so clever!

Welcome to Benburger Museum

Security check! Is everyone in place? The front door is now open. The early bird visitors rush in. Picking up museum guide books, some visitors begin a self-guided tour. Other visitors walk toward the audio carts, placed between the morning room and music room, to claim their audio.

"Good morning and welcome to Benburger Museum," said Lily.

"Put the orange cord over your head," Agnes said, as she handed the first visitor his audio. "Do you have a guide book?"

"I don't need one," the visitor assured Agnes. "I'm a pass holder and have been here many times."

"You will need a book, sir," said Lily. "It's a guide for your audio tour."

"My wife has one," said the visitor. "She can tell me what to do."

"I bet she would love too," thought Agnes.

Please go over to D.J. for your instructions," added Lily.

"Good morning, folks," said D.J. "Turn to page two in your museum guide book. Here you fine one of four maps to follow for your tour today. Please notice that every room has a number in a circle. These are your main room numbers and correspond to the key pad on your audio. We are now in room number one, the entrance hall."

"So, you press the room number and the green button?" questioned a visitor.

"No," said D.J. "Your units are turned on and are fully automatic. All you do is press the room number on the key pad and listen. After the information stops, simply walk to the next room and press that room's number to continue."

"What does the red button do?" asked another visitor.

"That's a pause button, Ma'am," said D.J. "You press it to pause while the program is running."

"So you press the red button to pause and the green button to begin again?" asked another visitor, eager to understand these complicated instructions.

"That is correct," said D.J.

Continuing, D.J. added, "Your volume buttons are on either side of the red button with yellow speaker symbols."

"Which way does the headset go on your head?" questioned a visitor.

"The wire side goes over your left ear, sir," said D.J.

"If you have to leave the house, you cannot take the audios with you," stated D.J. "Please take them to the small audio cart beside the front door and pick up a voucher. When you return, go to that same cart and pick up a fresh audio to continue your tour."

"Why would we want to leave the house?" asked one visitor, with a puzzled look on her face.

"Well, you might want to check your email," thought D.J. "Because there are no public rest rooms in Benburger Museum, one might need to leave and go to the stable next to the house, where public rest rooms are

located. The Horseshoe Cafe and Tack Room gift shop are also open for your convenience."

"If you have any audio problems," added D.J., "please find a host with a name tag. He, or she, will bring you a new one. You are now in room number one, the entrance hall. Press one on the audio keypad, listen, and then proceed to the formal dining room when the information stops. Enjoy your tour."

"So, you press the room number and then the green button to enter the information?" stated a visitor.

"Spot on!" exclaimed D.J. "Have a wonderful day."

We need new audios like last year! Our MP3 players are at least 10 years old and currently come in three health categories: well, sick, and hospice care. This creates a real challenge to maintain the players in good working condition. It also creates many fun images and expressions that we would like to share with our wonderful visitors, who put up with us and these audios on a daily basis. But, it is not in the best interest of hospitality.

You know something is up when you see a lady running toward the audio cart clutching her audio and headset with a frantic expression on her face. As you put on your best host smile you say, "May I help you?"

"Yes. My audio died," she exclaimed.

"I'm so sorry to hear that. Please know that in addition to this magnificent audio tour, we also offer scheduled audio funeral services held outside in the fountain garden. Please check with the host at the ticket counter by the entrance to Benburger Museum to make all the necessary arrangements. Music and flowers may be added for an additional fee."

This guest really looks unhappy.

"My audio skips," she exclaimed.

"How exciting," I replied. "You should see the ones that tap dance. On weekends we offer special audio dance programs, featuring professional audio groups. Tickets may be purchased at the front ticket counter. Be sure to catch my favorite group, the Tippy Tappy Toe Clogging Audios from Saluda!"

This next guest looks quite frustrated.

"Hi. My audio keeps repeating itself."

"How sad," I replied. "Audio dementia can be so disturbing. Security will be here shortly to whisk away this poor soul to our health maintenance department for special evaluation and treatment. In the meantime please accept one of our award winning audios for outstanding service and quality."

"May I help you, sir?"

"Yes. I only have sound out of one side of my headset."

"May I please see your ticket voucher," I asked. "Sir, I see that you purchased a half priced ticket which entitles you to one sided sound only. You do have a choice of the left or right side. We can make that adjustment here at the audio cart. For full stereo, please contact the ticket counter up front for further instructions. Have a wonderful day."

"My audio is scratchy," said the young girl with the pink tinted hair and pierced nose.

"We can take care of that," I added. "Our medical staff is quite informed with many varieties of itchy conditions that could cause a scratchy audio response. All audios and headsets are completely disinfected. They are properly cleaned between use and in the evening before bedtime. However, we never know when one of those rascals might enjoy the pleasures of an evening romp!"

Visitors often ask the most interesting questions, and sometimes receive interesting information from the museum hosts.

"How did the Benburgers live here with all these ropes blocking the entrance to each room?" inquired a visitor.

"These ropes were added long after the Benburger family lived here. They are used specifically to guide visitors through the museum house tour and protect all valuable items."

"Where is the ball room?" asked another visitor. "I know I saw one on my last visit."

"Benburger house does not have a ball room," said the host. "Archival documentation suggests that Mr. Benburger had no balls."

"Do those stairs go up?" asked a visitor, looking at the grand staircase.

"Yes," smiled a host. "The grand staircase goes up to the second and third floors. We also have a set of stairs that go down to the lower level."

"Where are they located?" questioned the visitor.

"Those stairs are located across from the grand staircase on the first floor level. Please be careful on the stairs."

"Did the Benburgers show indoor movies?" The visitor asked.

"Not to my knowledge, sir," said the host.

"Well, with the ticket counter up front, I thought maybe they sold tickets for show nights."

"Sir, the ticket counter was added after the house became a museum to accommodate visitors to purchase tickets and acquire information."

"Where are the secret passages?" The visitor asked.

"To my knowledge there are no secret passages in Benburger Museum," informed the host.

"That is hard to believe, ma'am," added the visitor.

"Why is that?" questioned the host.

"In a movie they made here in the museum several years ago, there were two con men that kept opening a concealed door leading into a secret passage."

"Some of that movie was filmed in an upstairs bedroom, sir. There is a door covered in the same wall paper as the room's walls. This gives the appearance of a concealed door which, I hate to tell you, leads into the bedroom closet and not into any secret passage."

"Well, I'm sure there must be one somewhere in the museum," stated the visitor.

One host was amused when a visitor asked, "Is this museum haunted?"

"Not to my knowledge, sir," answered the host. "Why do you ask?"

"Well, when I came up from the basement using the back stairs leading to the kitchen area, I am sure I heard voices coming from inside the turret wall."

"How interesting," said the host? "I must check this out. One never knows, does one?"

And, so it goes!

Christmas at Benburger Museum

Christmas at Benburger Museum is very special and one of Beatrice's favorite seasons of the year. It begins the first weekend in Advent with the Hanging of the Greens ceremony. A great deal of planning goes into how the ceremony is to be conducted. The order of the ceremony and special food items for the Horseshoe Cafe are top priority. Different varieties of ivy, mistletoe, and poinsettias begin arriving daily. Boughs of holly, fir, spruce, and pine are procured from the estate. Employees from the horticulture department scout out the forest areas to find that proper Yule log and Christmas fir tree to be placed in the formal sitting room. Garlands and wreaths are designed by the floral department with a special wreath for the front door. A new Christmas audio tour gives visitors insight into some of the Benburgers' favorite Christmas traditions. This is a busy time for all departments.

The ceremony is rather unique, based on long standing customs and current imagination. Visitors purchase tickets for the event and are asked to bring a home-made ornament to hang on the large Christmas fir tree in the formal sitting room. This custom dates back to medieval Germany, where Christmas trees were first used in paradise plays. The fir trees were decorated with apples, gilded nuts, dates, pretzels, and paper flowers. Those guests who bring paper ornaments to decorate the fir tree are encouraged to write a special wish for family and friends for Christmas and the New Year on the back of each ornament.

This year, music is being provided by the Octet Singers of Champion Community College. They always provide a wonderful assortment of Christmas carols to enhance the Hanging of the Greens ceremony. The singers are dressed in "Charles Dickens" era costumes, and visitors are given the option to join in the "dress up" fun. After the ceremony, visitors are invited to go back to the Horseshoe Cafe to partake of various hot drinks including spiced tea and, as my dear friend Fiona in England would say, "some sweeties to delight the soul."

One week to go before dramatic delirium weekend! Only first floor rooms are included in the Hanging of the Greens ceremony. The rest of the house is fully decorated with garlands, wreaths, kissing balls, candles, poinsettias, and decorated artificial trees. The only live Christmas tree is located in the formal sitting room. The stable, the Tack Room Gift Shop, and the Horseshoe Cafe are all decorated. Menus are updated at the Horseshoe Cafe to include special foods that are popular during this season. It is truly a festive time of the year with much excitement and anticipation.

The Hanging of the Greens Ceremony

It was a lovely evening, not too cold, but enough of a chill in the air to let one know that winter was waiting in the wings to emerge as its glorious self. All was ready in the Horseshoe Cafe for the evening's ceremony. Large baskets were placed near the entrance of the cafe for visitors to deposit their homemade Christmas ornaments. A small platform was installed inside the cafe for the Master of Ceremonies to stand on, to welcome visitors, and to explain the history behind the ceremony.

The first shuttle from the visitor parking lot arrived in front of Benburger Museum around 5:30 PM. Other shuttles followed shortly, until a rather large group was assembled in the Horseshoe Cafe. Promptly at 6:30, Jonathan Simms, curator of Benburger Museum and Master of Ceremonies, alerted the assembled visitors that the evening's ceremony was about to begin.

"Good evening and welcome to Benburger Estate," said Jonathan. "We have a very exciting Hanging of the Greens ceremony planned to usher in this Christmas season. Again, we are very fortunate to have with us Beatrice and George Benburger, represented by Darlene Sprinkle and Sam Goforth, from Guest Services. Beatrice and George look forward to being our hosts each year, leading our visitors through their house to enjoy the beautiful decorations and ceremonial customs."

"The Hanging of the Greens ceremony comes to us from England, where it had its origin in winter festivals long before the Christian era. Holly, ivy, and mistletoe were part of the original chosen greenery and were used to lift people's spirits, to know that spring was not far off. Boughs of holly were given as gifts to friends and family to protect against lightning strikes, and to ward off evil spirits. Ivy was held in high regard as a symbol of friendship and eternal life."

"Mistletoe held a special charm. Because this parasitic plant had no roots, it was thought to grow from heaven and have magical healing powers. In Scandinavia, mistletoe was dedicated to the Goddess of Love. The Norse people believed that this is how the custom of kissing under the mistletoe came about. A very nice custom indeed," exclaimed Jonathan. "Now it is my great pleasure to introduce you to Beatrice and George Benburger who are our guides for the Hanging of the Greens Ceremony this evening."

"Good evening," said Beatrice. "My husband George, indicating Sam, and I welcome all of you to participate in this exciting ceremony. We both look forward each year, to begin the Christmas season at Benburger Estate with the Hanging of the Greens ceremony."

"Yes, welcome to our home, and thank you for being here to celebrate with us," said George. "We have an exciting program planned with more history, customs, and music to dress our home in splendor for the holidays. First the Octet Singers will lead us to the front entrance of the house singing a new song. This song was written expressly for this occasion entitled <u>Christmas Is Near</u>."

Christmas Is Near

Ivy, mistletoe, and holly shout the news that Christmas is near.

Boughs of fir, pine, and spruce echo the news that Christmas is near.

Hang the wreaths and wrap the garlands, spread the news that Christmas is near.

Join the fun with music and dance; singing songs of good cheer.

Rejoice to know that Christmas is near.

Rejoice to know that Christmas is near.

See the house all bare and wanting,

Waiting for news that Christmas is near.

Bring the wreaths and bring the garlands.

Dress the lady in red and green with ribbons all a flaunting.

Rejoice to know that Christmas is near.

Rejoice to know that Christmas is near.

Come within and join the fun.

Hang the mistletoe on high.

Kiss the girls and pluck a berry,

To know that kissing will soon be gone.

Rejoice to know that Christmas is near.

Rejoice to know that Christmas is near.

Hark, the tree in glorious splendor,

Waiting for news that Christmas is near.

Dressed in garlands and glittering trinkets,

Light the tree for all to see.
Rejoice to know that Christmas is near.
Rejoice to know that Christmas is near.

There's the Yule log awaiting,
Announcing the news that Christmas is near.
Light the log to keep us warm and free from harm,
For this year and the next.
Rejoice to know that Christmas is near.
Rejoice to know that Christmas is near.

"After the ceremony at the front of the house, you will than be led into the entrance hall for another decorating experience," stated Beatrice. "From there we will proceed to all of the rooms on the first floor beginning with the formal dining room."

The guests assembled in front of the stable and were led by the Octet Singers to the front of Benburger Museum singing Christmas is Near. All gathered around the entrance while Beatrice and George Benburger prepared to begin the ceremony.

"I want to thank the floral staff and hosts for their tireless effort in bringing this ceremony to life," said Beatrice. "They are responsible for the lovely decorations we will be viewing this evening, beginning with garlands and wreaths to decorate the entrance to our lovely home."

"Garlands originally were prepared by intertwining holly and ivy to decorate the doorway entrance into one's home," stated George. "These garlands represented the unity of the dual halves of divinity. The holly represented the goddess or female and the ivy represented the consort to the goddess, and was therefore the masculine element."

"The holly wreath with its red berries dates back to at least 17th century England," said Beatrice, "and came to represent the crown of thorns worn by Christ, representing eternal life. This year the floral department has prepared garlands and several wreaths, to decorate our entrance columns, as well as a special wreath to decorate the front door."

As the Octet Singers performed the carol, The Holly and the Ivy, the floral department decorated the columns and front door of Benburger Museum. With the front entrance fully decorated, everyone prepared to enter the house to continue the ceremony. However, Beatrice stepped forward with some additional information.

"Continuing with past tradition, legend says that the first person, male or female, to enter the house bearing a holly branch rules the home for the rest of the year. Therefore, Mr. Benburger and I will now draw straws to see this wonderful custom come to pass. However, this will only pertain to this evening! I don't think we could manage a whole year!" Straws were drawn and Beatrice won the honor."Welcome to our home," invited Beatrice and George. Taking a holly branch from one of the hosts, Beatrice led the way into the entrance hall.

The Octet Singers burst forth with Deck the Halls as the guests filed into the entrance hall. Lighted garlands, hanging wreaths, glowing candles, and mistletoe kissing balls dressed the hall. Visitors echoed their heartfelt approval with thunderous applause and shouts of joy Mr. Benburger stepped forward to quiet the crowd. He was standing under a kissing ball.

"It seems that every custom is preceded by a legend," he said. "Kissing under the mistletoe is no exception. Originally, when a boy kissed a girl under the mistletoe, he plucked a white berry and gave it to her. When the berries were all gone, there was no more kissing. While we no longer pluck the berries, kissing under the mistletoe is a custom that will remain forever. There are a significant number of kissing balls hanging throughout our home. Kiss at your own discretion, but please, do not pluck the berries!"

George and Beatrice led the group into the formal dining room, where floral hosts were busy lighting the Christmas tree and arranging garlands. The dining table was decorated with poinsettias, assorted greenery, and candles to complement a large wassail bowl, the central focal point of the table. As the guests gathered around, George and Beatrice stood in front of the dining table.

"We would be remiss in welcoming all of you to our home, if we did not offer you a toast to good health, good fortune, and goodwill during this blessed season," exclaimed Beatrice. A host stepped forward, filled two ornate cups from the beautiful wassail bowl, and handed a cup to George and Beatrice. Turning to face the visitors, the Benburgers continued, "We salute you by saying, May your lives be filled with love, beauty, and joy this season and always."

As Beatrice and George exited the formal dining room through a door leading into the butler's pantry, the Octet Singers led the group down the hall into the small dining room singing We Wish you a Merry Christmas. Hosts lighted the Christmas tree and directed visitors around the room. The singing continued and was directed toward the door leading to the butler's pantry. After two choruses of "Bring Us Some Figgie Pudding," Beatrice and George emerged from the butler's pantry each carrying a tray of four small Figgie puddings. A pudding was given to each of the eight singers.

George explained, "This custom of giving was observed during the middle ages as a charitable gesture between the lord and lady of the manor. Food and drink were given to the locals in exchange for their blessing and goodwill. Therefore, we offer our blessing and goodwill to the Octet singers this evening for their beautiful music to enhance the Hanging of the Greens ceremony . . . their blessing to us and to all of our visitors."

From the small dining room, visitors were led into the morning room decorated in a homey atmosphere. A lighted Christmas tree, candles, poinsettias, personal mementos and photographs of the Benburger family enhanced the theme. As George and Beatrice entered the room, a host placed a vase of red roses on a table. Roses were Beatrice's favorite flower, and she always included them in her Christmas decor.

George and Beatrice took a seat across from one another. George picked up a newspaper and said, "Have you thought about Christmas gifts this year?"

"Indeed," said Beatrice. "As you know, we give Christmas gifts to the children of our servants every year. I always look forward to asking the parents what gift each child would like, finding the gifts to purchase, and wrapping them with the help of my wonderful team of ladies. It is most rewarding, and reminds me of purchasing Christmas gifts for our children, hoping that we make the right choices."

"Well, most of the time," added George. "There are always a few mishaps, but mostly we shrug them off. Christmas dinner mellows any disgruntled attitudes, especially with that last serving of mince pie. Well, my dear, let us go into the music room where the singers have a special program for us."

The guests were led into the music room decorated with an assortment of Christmas greenery and a lovely lighted Christmas tree decorated in a musical theme. The Octet Singers grouped around the piano and introduced their first song. It was <u>Lo, How a Rose E'er Blooming,</u> an old 15th century carol, based upon the eleventh chapter of Isaiah, verse 1: "And there shall come forth a rod out of the stem of Jesse, and a branch shall grow out of his roots." The inspirational harmony of the singers, as they expressed the message of this beautiful song, was appreciated by all.

"Our second song this evening was written by John Jacob Niles, often called the Dean of American

Balladeers. This song grew out of a true experience John had in the Appalachia town of Murphy, North Carolina, in July 1933. The Morgan family, all revivalists with no money, was just about to be ousted from Murphy, as they were living in the town square and came to be noted as a public nuisance. With no money to buy gas for the car to leave town, Annie Morgan stepped forward and sang the first three lines of

I Wonder as I Wander at twenty-five cents a performance to raise the necessary money to purchase gas for the car. John left with only three lines of a verse, some written notes, and an idea for this truly beautiful song we now sing for you. The first verse becomes the chorus in this arrangement. It depicts a young girl as she wanders under the sky wondering about the meaning of the birth of Jesus."

As the singing began, one of the female singers wandered over to a small table to the right of the piano and lit a candle. This was repeated after each verse, with another female singer going to the left of the piano to light another candle. With the last verse, the remaining two female singers each separated as they walked to the back of the music room and lighted several candles. With the last chores in place, all of the female singers came back to the piano, and the group ended the song. Everyone was transfixed with the mystical beauty of the experience. The applause was spontaneous. George and Beatrice next addressed the visitors from the entrance hall, inviting them to come into the library for another treat.

As the guests entered the library, the glow from the fireplace warmed the room and created an inviting atmosphere as a host lighted the Christmas tree in the background. In the center of the library was a gentleman sitting on a stool behind a podium.

"Welcome," said William Page. "I'm the historian for the Benburger Museum. This evening, I have chosen one of the Benburger children's favorite stories to share with you. It is about Gunter, a mouse, who claims to be very special. Gunter is special, but not in the way he perceives himself to be. Here is the story of Gunter the Frugal Mouse."

Gunter the Frugal Mouse

A long time ago, in a very worthy manor house, lived a mouse called Gunter. Now Gunter was not just any ordinary mouse. Oh, no. He was very frugal which set him apart from all the other mice, or so he thought. Gunter was born in this manor house, and took great pleasure in thinking he was very special because of his birthright. Many mice came from other circumstances and invaded the manor house, which made Gunter very upset. How dare they invade his territory! After all, he was very special.

Gunter's parents had died long ago, and he was now alone to roam around the house gathering the finest goodies from the kitchen, dining room, and wherever he could find a suitable morsel to add to his satchel. One could never have too many goodies, and he felt a sense of pride in his collectables: meat, cheese, grains, fruit, and an occasional drop of wine. Life was good, and Gunter enjoyed it to the fullest.

Gunter soon became a recluse and would only prowl around the house at odd times to avoid the other mice. He had nothing in common with them, so why should he bother to befriend them? After all, he was very special! As time went on, however, the other mice came together to discuss the likes of Gunter. To them, he was just a mouse. The only difference was that Gunter *thought* he was special. This made no sense to the rest of the mice. Why did he think he was so special?

A meeting of the Mouse Brotherhood was scheduled. After much discussion, the Host Mouse called for a committee to be formed to set a plan to bring Gunter into the Mouse Brotherhood. This organization was established by the mice to address special needs. Gunter certainly needed help. Being frugal was one thing, but being unfriendly was not acceptable.

A plan was set. The Brotherhood committee assigned certain duties to trained post mice. They were to be posted at various places throughout the manor house, during the day and evening, to determine Gunter's roaming patterns. Runner mice reported this information to the Host Mouse in charge. After a great deal of excitement, while checking last minute details, all was ready to launch "Gunter Rescue!"

The post mice scurried to their assigned stations, being careful to conceal their presence. Waiting was brutal, and the long hours of doing nothing seemed futile. To keep alert, each post mouse's position was changed every half hour. But they were trained to stand post and to be very observant to all details. Finally, in the kitchen storeroom area, Gunter was spotted. He seemed very sure of himself and not at all fearful of being caught. Procuring goodies was his specialty. Gunter's roaming patterns were noted throughout the house in great detail. Another meeting was scheduled to set the next stage of "Gunter Rescue."

After much discussion, it was determined that specially trained post mice were to be assigned to the most visited areas where Gunter roamed. They were to approach Gunter with kindness and offer assistance as determined by the rules of their training manual, with no exception. The second phase of Gunter Rescue was launched with a definite purpose . . . rescue the mouse!

Finally, Gunter was spotted in the dining room following a lovely meal with a suitable amount of top notch goodies to be procured. As Gunter filled his small satchel, he suddenly noticed a shadow crowding into his space. He spun around and faced a rather ominous mouse, but one with a kind face and non-threatening demeanor.

"Hello Gunter," said the post mouse. "You are indeed a very special mouse to gather such notable and delicious goodies in your satchel. Not everyone has this skill which, I imagine, has taken many years for you to develop. How special you are!"

Gunter was indeed startled to have anyone speak to him and to complement him on being special.

"Who are you, and how did you know my name?" questioned Gunter.

"My name is Sprout," said the post mouse. "Your name and skills are known throughout the house by all of the mice. You are greatly admired for your knowledge and expertise in gathering food. I came here from the country, because I always wanted to live in a manor house. While sprouted grains were my main country diet, my tastes have changed living here. I never knew such a variety of food was available for all to share."

Gunter was taken off guard and really did not know what to say. Did this mouse want to be his friend? How odd. He had certainly not gone out of his way to befriend any of the mice. Why did Sprout want to be his friend now?

"I was born in this manor house, and it has as very special meaning to me. I belong here. This is my home," stated Gunter.

"Even though we come from different beginnings, this is our home, too," said Sprout. "We each come from various backgrounds, and each mouse has his or her own special talent, which serves all of us by working together."

"What does that mean? Working together?" questioned Gunter. "I like to be on my own. I get more done that way. I don't bother you. You don't bother me. That's the way it is."

"That certainly is the way it is now," said Sprout. "But there is another way that makes life so much more meaningful and fun. Shortly after I arrived here, I became ill. Coming into such a big house, I did not know what to do, where to go, how to gather food, or anything. Then a group of wonderful mice came to my rescue. Those mice from health clinics went out and gathered herbs to cure my illness. Mice from hospitals nursed me back to health. Other country mice brought me food that I was used to eating. Scheduled mice checked on me daily and offered assistance when needed. It was a blessing. I would have never made it alone. Doing your own thing is good sometimes, but sharing your talents with others gives new meaning to a more productive life."

"I have a life," protested Gunter. "It's my life, and I like it … a lot!"

"I know you do," said Sprout. "That's very evident. All the mice watch you and notice your fear, doubt, and that creepy facade you present as *Lord Mouse of the Manor*! That is too funny. We get quite a laugh at your play acting."

"It is not play acting!" exclaimed Gunter. "I have a certain obligation to myself and my birthright. You are quite rude."

"Well," said Sprout. "Maybe it is time for you to experience a *rude awakening* to find out just who you really are. You might be surprised to find out that you are more of a special mouse than you think you are."

Gunter was stunned. "You mean I might be more special than I am? How is that possible?"

"I would like to introduce you to our group called the Mouse Brotherhood. Everyone is anxious to meet you. You could see how special we all are, and how well we work together creating many wonderful experiences in this old house we all call home."

Gunter had some reservations about going to any meeting. I might as well go, he thought. I've nothing to lose, right? I will give them my name, house history, and birthright information. That should count for something. This *Lord Mouse of the Manor* is ready for the challenge. Let it begin!

The meeting took place in a storage room in the basement of the house. Everyone was excited to finally meet Gunter, and to see just who this mouse really was. The meeting started at seven p.m. After a call to order by the Host Mouse, everyone looked around. No Gunter!

"We have other business to address," stated the Host Mouse. "We will continue until Gunter arrives. Sprout has gone looking for him."

Sprout found Gunter hiding in a corner of the basement trying to decide if he really wanted to attend the meeting. What if they made fun of him? What if they called him names and bullied him? There were a lot of questions running through Gunter's mind and none of them very nice. Gunter had never really been unkind to any of the mice, so why should they be unkind to him? Yet he was very fearful of this new situation he faced. This was definitely not within his comfort zone.

"There you are," shouted Sprout. "Getting cold feet? There's nothing like four cold feet to drain one's self-confidence. Wait until your tail goes numb!"

Gunter turned pale with fright.

"Just kidding," laughed Sprout. "Come on. Everyone is really anxious to meet you, and I promise, I will be by your side all evening even if you might not want me to be there. "

"I do! I do!" exclaimed Gunter trembling with the thought of being alone. "Please don't leave me. I appreciate your kindness."

"Hey. It sounds like we just eliminated the first step in the rude awaking saga of the *Lord Mouse of the Manor*. Come on," said Sprout. "The meeting has already started."

The business meeting was drawing to a close when the door opened and in walked Sprout and Gunter. The crowd grew silent as the Host Mouse greeted the two mice. Then the whole room exploded into applause and mouse squeaks. Gunter was taken by surprise and really did wonder if his tail would go numb with all of the excitement. He had never witnessed anything like it. In some ways it was totally frightening, and in other ways it was very special. He was so glad that Sprout kept his word and stayed with him throughout the evening. All of the mice introduced themselves and gave their history before coming to the manor house. It was amazing to witness all of the talent in the room. In addition to those in the health field, some mice were from farms and knew proper mouse nutrition. Others came from business backgrounds and knew how to conduct the administrative functions of the Mouse Brotherhood. Other mice came from teaching backgrounds and were instrumental in teaching young mice how to understand themselves and life. Everyone had their own special talent.

Slowly Gunter came to understand that all of these talents were needed to survive. While being frugal was a talent, his special talent of how to roam and scout for food was very important. Soon he was teaching other mice this skill, and he was learning many things from them. He soon became a trusted friend to all. Life took on new meaning for Gunter.

He came to realize that the diversities of life offer many talents which, through love, kindness, and support, create a living expression of life that is a blessing to all.

The story was well received with much clapping and shouts of appreciation. The lovely message of the story with its blessing set the tone for the Christmas season: love, acceptance, and kindness to all. Mr. Page rose from his stool, and announced that all should now proceed into the formal sitting room for the conclusion of this evening's Hanging of the Greens ceremony.

As the visitors filed into the formal sitting room the hosts and floral staff were just putting the last of the homemade ornaments on the tree. The mantle over the fireplace was decorated with greenery including mistletoe and holly. Candles were on each end of the mantle ready to be lighted. There was no fire in this fireplace.

Finally, Mrs. Benburger stepped forward and said, "In keeping with the German tradition of decorating a fir tree with homemade ornaments, we salute you the visitors and staff for this wonderful expression of your love and support. Mr. Benburger and I have some of our family decorations that we would now like to add to the tree as the Octet Singers sing, <u>Oh Christmas Tree</u>."

During the singing, Beatrice and George went over to the tree and placed their family ornaments on several branches. As soon as they finished, the tree was lighted.

As the song ended, visitors expressed their approval, knowing that their home made decorations added to the beauty of this special tree.

George Benburger stepped forward to explain the custom of the Yule log.

"I imagine that most of you have noticed that we do not have the fireplace lit in this room. We will end our Hanging of the Greens ceremony with the lighting of the Yule log. This custom is one of the most ancient of Christmas traditions dating back to the late twelfth century in Germany. It was thought that the burning of the Yule log brought prosperity for the coming year. In Ireland a Christmas candle was lit to usher in the holiday season. Tonight we light the Yule log, represented by the gas logs in this fireplace, as hosts light the two Christmas candles on each end of the mantle. But first, Beatrice and I would like to recite a poem, The Yule Log written by Robert Herrick during the seventeenth century. As a token of remembrance for this custom, two men from engineering will bring in the Yule log and place it on the hearth in front of the fireplace."

Beatrice began the poem by saying,

"Come; bring with a noise,
my merry, merry boys,"

George continued:

"The Christmas log to the firing;
While my good dame, she
Bids ye all be free"

At this point, two men from engineering came through the crowd carrying the Yule log on their shoulders. The Octet Singers shook bells while the visitors cheered and clapped their approval. The two men laid the log on the hearth in front of the gas logs. Several members of the floral staff decorated the log with garlands of pine, holly, and mistletoe. Beatrice and George continued reciting the poem together:

"And drink to your hearts desiring,
with the last year's brand.
Light the new block, and

For good success in his spending,
on your Psalteries play,
that sweet luck may come while the log is tending."

While hosts lighted the two Christmas candles on the mantle, the two men from engineering lit the gas logs. Every one gazed at the beauty of the ambiance within the room: the glowing fireplace, the decorated tree, the beautiful candlelit mantle, and the Yule log. The Octet Singers gathered around the fireplace and sang <u>Carol of the Bells</u> using bells to embellish the joyful expression of the song.

With this, the ceremony ended. George and Beatrice thanked the visitors for sharing in the Hanging of the

Greens ceremony to decorate their home. They wished everyone a Merry Christmas and a prosperous New Year.

Some visitors walked to the second and third floors to view the rest of the house's decorations. Some walked to waiting shuttles to go back to their cars. Other visitors headed to the Horseshoe Cafe for refreshments. Everyone left radiating the spirit of the season.

A Benburger Christmas "Ah Ha" Moment

Beginning the first week in Advent, different instrumental groups perform daily in the museum music room. Choirs join the instrumental groups on weekends, for the Festival of Lights. This festival is an evening function consisting of touring the museum in a home-like atmosphere viewing the Christmas decorations, lighted candles, and burning fire places. Lily, my audio buddy, and I like most of the daytime instrumental groups, especially the harp. We also like the trio of violin, guitar, and flute. A more mountain flavor is offered by the violin, guitar, and dulcimer ensemble. We even like the gentleman who plays the Sitar. The music is beyond our understanding, but it offers a pleasant and soothing sound. However, there is one group that drives us nuts . . . the two soprano flutes! We don't know what they play because it always sounds like finger exercises and running scales. We have dubbed them, *the dueling flutes!*

"They sound like two birds in heat!" Exclaimed lily!

"They had better get a room, or they're going to be two dead birds in heat!" I added.

"It just makes you want to go up to the third floor and drop a bag of marbles down the grand staircase," said Lily.

"A few cymbal crashes would really be exciting!" I exclaimed.

Lily and I both had been in community theatre for many years, hence our vivid imaginations. We listened to the musical offerings daily and soon got tired of hearing the same groups, the same music, and especially the dueling flutes. There had to be another form of entertainment that was really exciting, different, and over the edge. On the days we worked together, we spent hours mentally exploring the possibilities of ideas that would be outstanding. One morning, as we were deep in thought, a gentleman came into the museum on a Segway PT unit. Our jaws dropped as we watched the gentleman navigate around the first floor of the museum. He was amazing. He went forward. He backed up. He turned to the right. He turned to the left. He slowed down. He sped up. He turned in a circle. And then, there it was! An idea of such magnitude and proportion, combining the melding of synaptic thought with emotional brilliance, sending a charge of electricity through our bodies leaving us breathless. We would create and perform a Segway Ballet!

Preparations for the Ballet

Neither Lily nor I had ever had any training on how to operate a Segway, a self-balancing personal transportation device with two wheels. I mean, we both have problems just walking around the museum! Could we master the segway in a rather short period of time? There was so much to think about and so much to do to achieve our goal.

It seemed the best time to perform this ballet was during the Twelfth Night Festival held at the museum January fifth. This festival represented the ending of Christmastide, or the Twelve Days of Christmas, from December twenty-fifth through January fifth, leading into Epiphany on January sixth. This was a time of merry making, good food, and celebration. First of all we needed approval from HR to perform such an unusual program. Then we needed to find some company that sold Segways and offered training to master the art of Segway movement. Later the selection of music, choreography, and costumes would be addressed. Our minds were full of ideas, and plans were made to carry them out. The hardest part was finding time to accomplish all of this while working. But, we would find a way!

We grabbed the Yellow Pages and looked up Segway Equipment and Training. A Mr. Ziggy Albright was listed under Albright Human Transport Systems, Inc. as a Segway rep selling Segways as well as giving lessons in

Segway movement. This was mainly geared for business purposes, of course. "Wait until he learns what we want to do!" giggled Lily. Lily and I called to make an appointment on our day off for Wednesday next at 10:00. The meeting was just for consultation, and to look at a Segway that we could use for our ballet. This had to be a most unusual request for Ziggy!

Sylvia, Ziggy's receptionist, greeted us cordially and invited us to either have a seat or take a look at the Segway units in the showroom. Mr. Albright would join us shortly. We chose to look at the various Segways. Hushed chitchat, looks of awe, and utter amazement followed, as we examined each Segway trying to gather some understanding of just what we were looking at and how it might work.

With a jolting "Hello D.J. and Lily," Ziggy popped into the showroom to join us. He was the usual enthusiastic sales rep, full of charisma and charm, with a gleam in his eye that could sell funeral plans to the deceased, non-refundable. A little overweight with receding sandy gray hair, Ziggy asked, "What can I do for you folks today?"

"Well," sparkled Lily. "We are interested in looking at indoor Segways for a very special purpose."

"That would be the i2 series," said Ziggy. "Segways in this model category are used mainly indoors and outdoors under certain conditions. The x2 series is used mostly for outside activity. It looks like the basic i2 model could serve your purpose. It is easy to operate. It can go fast or slow, forward and backward, right and left, and turn in place. We also have the i2 Commuter model designed to run errands both indoors and out. The i2 Cargo model can carry small cargo in specially designed storage bags. I'm sorry, where did you say you were employed?"

"We are employed at Benburger Museum as audio hosts," stated D.J "Have you ever been to the museum, during the Christmas season? We have two beautiful festivals that visitors always enjoy."

"No. I can't say that I have. I'm not much into museums. Hunting and fishing are my things. Are you here representing the museum to purchase one or more Segways? The proper model or models depend on the purpose for which they will be used. How will they be used?" asked Ziggy.

Lily turned a little pale, but regained her courage and composure stating, "We do represent the museum in a very special way." She laid out the whole plan of why she and D.J. were there, to choose two Segways to perform a unique ballet during the Twelfth Night Festival at the museum.

"Mr. Lee Summers, our Special Events HR representative, has given us permission to perform the Segway ballet under certain conditions. We are not to purchase any Segways, but the museum would pay Albright Human Transport Systems, Inc. to rent two indoor Segways including a series of instructions on how to operate them. There would be a contract to sign between you and the museum for this purpose, including insurance necessary to protect your assets and your company. Liability insurance would be provided by the museum to protect D.J. and myself against any injuries that might occur during the training period."

The silence was deafening! It was Ziggy's time to turn a little pale, and he almost fell off one of his Segways trying to understand just what Lily had laid out for him. For a moment everyone just looked at each other waiting for Ziggy to say something. Ziggy finally came back to some kind of reality, cleared his throat, and proceeded to speak in a whisper-like version of his usual speaking voice. His sales persona had slipped a bit, and he stammered around trying to find some meaningful words to express himself.

"Is this for real? Have you lost your mind? Why should I even consider such a request? Segways are used mainly for business purposes, with the exception of the x2 outdoor series. I don't think I can do this. Why would you even think that I might go along with this crazy idea?" By this time Ziggy's sales persona had returned, and he was not a happy camper!

"First of all," said D.J. "The idea is not crazy. Maybe it is time for you to think outside the box and consider new avenues for the sale of your Segways. I'm not at all sure that sales have been that great for you this year, which is drawing to a close in a very few weeks. While you always rely on companies for the major sales of your Segways, how many of the public even know what a Segway is, the different purposes for its use, and how one works? This could be a great opportunity for Albright Human Transport Systems, Inc. to educate the public and possibly increase your sales. We can help you with that."

The words, "increase sales" brought Ziggy back to reality. "How could you help me increase sales?" questioned Ziggy.

"There are several things one might consider," suggested D.J. "The museum is always looking for ways to offer visitors outstanding programs, not only for their enjoyment, but also for educational purposes. I think a great way to introduce Segways to the public is to create a Segway Tour at the museum. The x2 outdoor models would be used for that purpose, I assume? The museum would purchase several Segways and have their employees take your training course to implement the tour program. The museum has been considering the establishment of outdoor programs to provide visitors with activities, other than just going into the museum. The Segway tour program could be the first one considered, with Segways provided by Ziggy Albright!"

More silence followed, but this time one could hear the wheels turning in Ziggy's head as he processed D.J.'s rather ingenious outline for a new area of growth for Albright Human Transport Systems, Inc. Finally, Ziggy said, "Come into my office. Let's explore all of the possibilities. I think you may have a great idea there. I never thought of Segway Tours. I never thought of a ballet, either. What a wild idea!"

An hour later, with a phone call to Mr. Summers to verify Lily and DJ's request to rent two Segways, contract information and arrangements for training were sealed for the Twelfth Night program. Ziggy and Mr. Summers were to meet the next day at the museum to sign the contract and discuss the possibility of a Segway tour at Benburger Museum. On the way out, Sylvia set up training schedules to begin right away as time was of the essence. We were to wear casual clothing and non-slip shoes. Helmets would be provided to guard against any falls until we became familiar with how the Segway moved.

The morning had been exhausting for both Lily and D.J. "I feel like going home and sleeping for a month," said Lily. "I'm absolutely drained!"

"Yeah, me too," said D.J. "Wish we could be at the meeting with Ziggy and Mr. Summers tomorrow. I cannot thank Mr. Summers enough for allowing us to perform this ballet and working out the details with Ziggy. The possibility of establishing a Segway tour at Benburger Museum is totally awesome. I am anxious to learn the final outcome of that idea."

"That was a brilliant idea you came up with," said Lily. "How did you think of that?"

"I don't know. It just popped into my head. I think the museum needs to expand its programs, and this is one way to accomplish that. We will see what happens. I'm going home. Swanson and I will have a lot to talk about. Call you later to discuss music and costumes."

"Bye," said Lily. "Talk to you soon. Give Swanson a big ol' hug from Aunt Lily."

"Will do," laughed D.J.

Ziggy did keep his promise to meet with Mr. Summers the next day. All details were worked out for the program. A contract was signed to clinch the deal for the Segway ballet including liability insurance for Lily and D.J. They further discussed the idea of establishing a Segway tour at the museum. Ziggy was asked to be on the committee to advise Benburger Museum on which Segways to purchase and how the tour should be established. The administrative offices, being located on the second floor of the stable, brought up the idea of having a commuter Segway going between the stable and the museum. After lunch at the Horseshoe Cafe, Mr. Summers took Ziggy on a tour of the Benburger Museum, his first time in any museum. Ziggy's eyes were opened, and he became totally immersed in the history of the Benburgers. He marveled at how Mr. Benburger made his fortune selling boeuf burgers!

Time was of the essence to get everything completed for Twelfth Night. It seemed liked there were four things to accomplish: learn how to handle the Segway, choose music, establish choreography, and select costumes. That certainly took up every day of the next four and a half weeks. Not much wiggle room there.

Our first training session was to learn how the Segway worked and to experience all of its movements. Mr. Rodney Pimm was our instructor. He informed us that the most outstanding feature of the Segway was its balancing ability. He compared it to the human body. If you leaned forward, you probably would not fall because the fluid in your inner ear would shift, and you would automatically put a leg forward to stop the fall. If you kept leaning forward, you would automatically walk to keep from falling. The difference with the Segway would be that it has wheels instead of legs, motors instead of muscle, a collection of microprocessors instead of a brain, a set of sophisticated tilt sensors instead of inner ear fluid, and an operator control system to accomplish all of the various moves. In order to move forward or backward on a Segway, lean slightly forward and slightly backward. The tilt sensors alert the Segway to move its wheels in the proper direction to achieve movement. When you lean forward, the motors spin both wheels forward to keep you from tilting over. Leaning backward allows the motors to spin the wheels backward. To move right or left, the handlebar controls move one wheel faster than the other to make the turn. The operator control system also allows the Segway to turn in a circle by rotating the wheels in opposite directions. "This is all you need to know about the Segway," said Rodney. "In fact, forget most of it, and concentrate on how to operate the Segway. This is best done by experiencing how it moves. So, follow me, and we will get started."

Because Benburger Museum has wood floors, Rodney led us to the training room with wooden floors. He showed us how to turn on the Segway by inserting the black electronic key into its port. The first beep initiated the beginner mode. This turned the controller panel on to move the Segway forward and backward, and activated the handlebar unit to turn the Segway left and right. Next he pressed the control panel, and the second beep brought up a smiley face to say that the Segway was now stable, balanced, and ready to ride.

"You have chosen to train on wood floors, so first I will show you how to move the segway in its various moves," said Rodney. "Then we will have you put on your helmets to begin your training." Lily and I spent more than an hour learning how to initiate the various moves, getting familiar with the unit, and gaining more confidence in ourselves. It was an awesome experience and a little nerve racking, to say the least. Lily and I loved the thrill of actually controlling the Segway in its various movements. We wondered if the gentleman who came into the museum had felt the same way. With the training sessions in place, our next step was to choose a theme for the ballet, pick music, and find a choreographer.

Later that evening, I called Lily to discuss a theme and music for our ballet. Her sparkling voice greeted me with, "Hi Cuddles. I have been thinking about a theme and music for our ballet. It has to be very special in every way. I spent the afternoon on the internet exploring ballet themes and music. There was so much to choose from it made me dizzy with excitement! Have you thought of anything?"

"Yes, I have a few things in mind," said D.J. "What have you come up with?"

"Well," gushed Lily. "I thought of an operatic theme, and came up with a piece from <u>The Nutcracker Suite</u> called, *The Dance of the Reed Flutes*. Wouldn't it be just too cool to dedicate our program to the dueling flutes?"

"How funny is that," laughed D.J. "However, I feel that we need to keep it simple as we have a little over four weeks to make this happen. We have lots to do in addition to working at the museum. Right now, we have Segway movements to master, music to choose, costumes to consider, and dance choreography to learn. That's a lot to accomplish in such a short time. But we can do it!"

"Hmm," said Lily. "I understand your point, so what's your plan?"

"Well," said D.J. "Since we are performing during the Twelfth Night Festival, why don't we use that as our theme, and look for some music to fit that type of celebration."

"I like that. So what do you have in mind?" requested Lily.

"While perusing the internet, I came across the *Elf Dance* by Hans Gustafsson in his <u>Wellness Music Sampler</u> CD. It seems that he took his inspiration for this music during a retreat in the Scandinavian countryside. On line, you can enjoy both the pictures of the beautiful Scandinavian scenery as well as the music. It is truly beautiful. You can just picture a dance unfolding to his music. It is free flowing and would lend itself to the type of Segway movements we are learning."

"Wow," said Lily. "You have really thought this through, and it does sound enchanting. Can't wait to hear the CD and see the pictures. Maybe we can create a slide show on a screen behind us as we danced?"

"That's a great idea," agreed D.J. "Not sure we have time to put that together this time, but save that thought. Maybe we can include that for another program in the future. In the meantime, please listen to the music, and let me know what you think. The CD needs to be purchased right away. Now, who are we going to have as our choreographer?"

"Back to the Yellow Pages," said Lily. "Guess we need to look under dance studios and contact some to see who might be interested in choreographing a ballet on a Segway. You know, it seems to me in talking to Mr. Summers about our ballet, he contacted a modern dance group to perform at the Twelfth Night evening program in the museum. Maybe they would be interested in choreographing our dance?"

"That's a great idea. I will call Mr. Summers to see what group he contacted. It would be good to engage a group that is already performing. They can give us a lot of support and correct any last minute changes, which I hope will not be necessary," added D.J.

"Good," said Lily. "In the meantime I will listen to the music and get back to you."

"Thanks for going along with me on the theme and music idea," said D.J. "I think when you hear the music;

you will be able to visualize the dance. We will discuss costumes later. Have a great evening and get some much needed rest. We have lots to do."

I talked to Mr. Summers the next day and got the name and phone number of the dance group called, The Adepts. Being a modern dance group, I thought their choreographer might actually be interested in staging our Segway performance. I called and talked with Annabelle Morrison and explained the whole story of how Lily and I came up with the idea of a Segway ballet. Again, there was a pause to let this information sink in. Then Annabelle said, "That could be quite an interesting challenge because dance, and in particular ballet, has to do with foot, leg, and body movement in various dance positions for both female and male dancers. Since the Segway would take the place of foot and leg movement, the upper body would have to be an extension of the Segway to move the dance forward to conclusion. Have you chosen a theme and some music for the ballet?"

"Yes," said D.J. "As we are performing during the Twelfth Night Festival at the Benburger Museum on January 5th, Lily and I have chosen this festival as the theme for our dance. I like the music *Elf Dance* by Hans Gustafsson from his Wellness Music Sampler CD. It seems to flow nicely and would lend itself to the various Segway movements we are learning. You can listen to this on the internet. Are you familiar with this piece of music?"

"No," said Annabelle. "I will listen to it and see if this piece lends itself to creating our dance. Have you thought of any particular characters that might fit the music and dance theme? This would help us with the choreography and the costumes."

"At first, I tried to think of a missing character, not included during the Christmas season at the museum or during Twelfth Night, and came up with an elf. So I looked for elf dance music. Then when I heard the *Elf Dance* by Gustafsson, I liked it immediately. The more I listened; the one thing that came to my mind was a free spirit moving to the rhythm of life. Because of this, the elf character was cancelled. Oh, I forgot to tell you. There are pictures of the Scandinavian countryside projected during the playing of the music. I think when you see and hear the two venues together you will understand the flow of life that I am talking about."

"Sounds fascinating," said Annabelle. "I look forward to hearing the music and seeing the pictures. The idea of a free spirit is excellent. One can have a lot of freedom to express life and movement with this concept. What are you and Lily doing right now to prepare for your ballet?"

"We are training at Albright Human Transport Systems, Inc. to learn the various Segway movements. Are you familiar with how a Segway moves?"

"No," said Annabelle. "Not really."

"The unit can move forward, backward, to the right, to the left, and in a circle. You can go in a straight line or create angle movements forward and backward, but not side to side. Perhaps you could come over to our next session and watch as we demonstrate these movements?"

"When will you be having your next training session?" asked Annabelle

"Actually, we will be practicing tomorrow morning at 10:00. Can you join us then?" asked D.J.

"Yes, I can," said Annabelle. "In the meantime, I will listen to the music and get some idea of how this piece sounds, to see if it might work for us. Give me the address of Albright Human Transport Systems, Inc. and your phone number, and I will see you at ten AM."

"Thanks," said D.J. "Lily and I look forward to meeting you, and thank you for your interest in choreographing our ballet."

All of us met at Ziggy's the next morning. I introduced Annabelle to Lily and Rodney. Both Lily and Annabelle had listened to the music sampler and liked the wonderful sound, tone, beat, and rhythm. All agreed that it was a good choice, and Lily was inspired by the idea of a free spirit moving to the rhythm of life. Lily and I put on our helmets and proceeded to demonstrate the various Segway movements, so Annabelle could visualize creating a dance choreography involving a PT unit. Lily and I proceeded to put our Segways through their various moves: forward, backward, angled side movements, right, left, and a circle. Annabelle took notes while viewing the demonstration, gathering ideas for the choreography. With the legs and feet more or less stabilized, a lot of movement would have to be added to upper body, arms, and head to create a dance accentuating the various Segway moves. This was a real challenge, but one that Annabelle looked forward to. "Just another prop to work with," she said. "Now we have to think about costumes to enhance two free spirits moving to the rhythm of life."

I turned to Lily and Annabelle for costume ideas. That was not my expertise for sure! Lily wanted something grand and elegant. Annabelle wanted something simple and flowing. After much discussion and debating, Annabelle envisioned Lily in a simple moss green dress undergarment, rather form fitting, with a boat style neck and full length sleeves to each wrist. The dress was to end just above her ankles keeping in mind the wheels on either side of the foot platform of the Segway. Even though there were wheel fenders on the inside of each wheel attached to the foot platform, dress length was an important issue. Because upper body, arm, and head movements were going to be important in the dance chorography, Annabelle suggested a white cape of a light, flowing fabric be attached to the moss green undergarment dress with pendants attached to each shoulder and arm to accentuate arm and upper body movement. In keeping with the Twelfth Night theme, Lily was to wear a crown of faux ivy, holly, and mistletoe attached to a wig of long flowing hair or at least some added hair pieces. Black shoes completed the ensemble. A beauty to behold!

I was the next victim of choice! Again, thinking of body movement, Annabelle suggested that I wear a pair of darker green tights with Renaissance style boots laced up on each side just below the knee. Over this was to be a white peasant style shirt/tunic, upper thigh length, with full sleeves drawing attention to arm movements. A laced vest of a rust-brown color was to be worn over the shirt. A cap with a feather completed my outfit. Not too shabby for D.J. Cuddles!

Both Lily and I were excited about Annabelle's costume ideas. She suggested that Lily begin to practice on the Segway wearing a long skirt with the black shoes she would wear during the performance. As the chorography progressed, the cape-dress would be added later. For the moment, I was to wear plain trousers, a peasant style shirt with full sleeves, and regular shoes.

The next big project was choreography. Annabelle said that she would have this ready in the next few days for us to review. Then another adventure would begin. Needless to say, Lily and I were quite nervous, and we began to wonder if senility had affected our rational thinking? No! Creative thinking was one of our passions. We just never thought where it might lead! What would Swanson think? Don't ask!

We did not hear from Annabelle for several days, and Lily and I began to panic over the lack of choreography for the ballet. We continued our lessons to perfect the Segway movements even taking a few risks to be creative ourselves. After today's Segway session we went to have a little lunch. As we talked about the choreography, my cell phone rang. Annabelle said that she had put some ideas together and could we meet? Having the afternoon free, Lily and I hurried over to Annabelle's studio.

Annabelle greeted us warmly and seemed very excited to show us the choreography she had put together for our ballet. We went into her studio and sat around a table. There was a chalk board close by for diagramming dance movements. Annabelle continued, "This music is very mesmerizing and lends itself toward meditation. For dance, however, one has to really keep focused not to succumb to this influence but to concentrate on counting in 4/4 time. Your choreography is a combination of Segway movement and body movement flowing together. We first start with Segway movement. Then we stop the Segway and continue with upper body movement. This transformation from Segway movement to body movement is the real critical aspect of the ballet. We cannot lose the illusion of flowing movement. From what Rodney showed me, as you stop the Segway, your knees are slightly bent. This would create an upward flowing movement as you stand up to continue with body, arm, and head movements. It is not just Segway movement first and body movement second, but a continual movement that is ever present and never stops. This will take practice. At first you will naturally tend to do the two types of movement separately, but as you get into the essence of the music and gain confidence, the flow will become one continuous movement and will be breathtaking. Nothing like this has ever been done. What a brilliant idea!"

While the idea was brilliant, Lily and I wondered just how brilliant we were in putting together this whole dance with a little over two and a half weeks to go. Annabelle knew she was working with two amateurs with grandiose ideas, so she was prepared to weather the storm, so to speak. Having been to the Benburger Museum with her dance troupe to see the entrance hall and how much space they would have for their dances, Annabelle already knew the layout. To begin the ballet, Lily was to come out of the morning room and D.J. was to come out of the library both meeting in front of the music room. Then they were to come down the center of the entrance hall, do a half circle, and face one another. From that position the dance would begin.

We spent the next two weeks rehearsing at Ziggys daily or evenings as work allowed. It was exhausting, but the adrenal rush of it all kept us going. Everything was finally coming together – the costumes, the Segway and dance movements, all set to the wonderful music we had chosen. Annabelle was truly excited and praised us for achieving so much in such a short period of time. With only three days to go before the Twelfth Night Festival, our rehearsals were moved into the museum in the evenings after closing. On some evenings we shared rehearsal time with Annabelle's dance troupe and the Allegro Instrumental Ensemble. While everyone had performance jitters, the whole atmosphere was amazingly serene and focused. It was a beautiful experience for all.

Twelfth Night Festival

January fifth finally arrived. It was a lovely day and almost too warm for this time of the year. Weather predictions were uncertain for the evening, however, as a cold front was moving in. All preparations for the festival were in place. Outside the stable, on either side of the walkway to the museum, tents were decorated with ribbons and garlands. This created a festive atmosphere for vendors to sell their wares. Some sold food and drink. Others sold everything from masks, festival clothing decorated with many colored strips of fabric, wigs, jester hats, ribbon favors, noise makers, hobby horses, and wooden swords for the mock mummer's battles. Children enjoyed the local artists offering face painting and hair tinting. The Tack Room gift shop and the Horseshoe Cafe were open all day to accommodate visitor's needs.

Just outside, to the left of the stable, was a large performance tent with a stage at the far end. This year, a troupe of 20 actors from a local community theatre, were engaged to perform skits including vaudeville acts and slapstick comedy. Singers, instrumental groups, magicians, and a band of mummers completed the list of tent performers. Outside performers included unicyclists, jugglers, clowns, and jesters. The festival began at two o'clock with outdoor activities ending at six. Then, everyone was to gather in the performance tent to receive further instructions for the evening's festivities inside the museum entrance hall.

This was an exciting day. Locals and out of town visitors always looked forward to this festival each year. By one o'clock, crowds began to gather along the festival route from the stable to the museum entrance and surrounding grassy areas. Vendors checked last minute preparations to open at two PM. Inside the performance tent, stage managers checked the order of performance times for the various groups including props, scenery, music, costumes, lighting, and any changes noted. Precisely at two, the festival began.

With a crash of cymbals, followed by yells and cheers, the entire ensemble of performers emerged from the stable in various costumes. They pranced along the festival parade route to the sounds of a New Orleans style jazz band, leading the way from the stable to the museum entrance. Here Mr. Summers, in charge of the festivities, emerged from the museum and welcomed all to the Twelfth Night Festival. After a short speech, the jazz band led the group back along the parade route to the stable to check leader boards for daily activities and performance times. The museum followed its regular schedule, closing at four-thirty to prepare for the evening's programs. The Twelfth Night Festival had begun and would continue well into the evening. Everything was right on schedule.

One addition this year to the festivities is the introduction of a troupe of performers called mummers, or guisers; meaning performing in disguise. The term "mumming" has its origin in the British Isles and refers to the performance of seasonal folk plays, originally performed in the street or in people's houses. They were later performed in public houses called pubs. In England today, many mummer plays are still performed outside in the street with crowds of onlookers urging the battle on. The plays are based on the two themes of duality and resurrection. In the play, one or more people or groups, representing good and evil, perform a mock battle with swords. Someone is slain, and a doctor is called in to administer a "magic potion" to revive the wounded back to life. Then, one of the characters calls on the audience to collect money to pay the doctor. All are saved, the doctor is paid at the last minute, and a blessing is given to all for the special season it represents. Enjoy this modern version of a mummers play written in traditional rhyming verse for our Twelfth Night festival.

Mummers Play

Cast of Characters:

Father Christmas
Old Bessie
Freddy, the Kindly Fool
Sir Falcon Knight and three gang members
Sir Raven Knight and three gang members
Dr. Goodly Pure
Lady May, Freddy's wife

(Father Christmas enters and comes to the center of the stage facing the audience.)

Father Christmas:

In come I, called Father Christmas.
Welcome here, or welcome not.
I hope the name of Father Christmas,
Will never be forgot.
Christmas comes but once a year.
Pray, be ye good or maybe not?
It's up to you, but never fear,
No one will ever be forgot.
So mind ye what I say.
Come, Old Bessie and clear the way.

(Enter Old Bessie with a broom)

Old Bessie: (Sweeping with her broom)

Here am I, Old Bessie with my broom.
Sweeping all around I go,
Making for a pretty room,
To give much space for this dumb show!

(Enter Freddy the Kindly fool)

Fool I may and fool I might,
But this kind fool is rather bright.
I bring ye friends, or maybe not,
Oh, how to judge this sorry lot?

(Enter Sir Falcon Knight and three gang members)

Sir Falcon Knight:

Here am I Sir Falcon Knight.
Me and my gang are here tonight,
With swords and rapier in sight.
We come to fight all those who jeer,
For we are strong and have no fear!

(The audience jeers with boos and hissing sounds)

(Enter Sir Raven Knight with three gang members)

Sir Raven Knight:

Here am I Sir Raven Knight.
My gang and I are here to fight.

The Sword Dance is our form of battle,
So, gather 'round and take your place,
And stop this silly foolish prattle.
We start with swords upheld in place.

(As the music starts for The Sword Dance, the
audience shouts and claps, to show their approval as the
mock sword battle begin between the Falcon and Raven
gangs. Freddy tries to join the fight, and is stabbed at the
end of the dance.)

Father Christmas:

Doctor! Doctor! Is there a doctor to be found,
To treat this man whose wound is quite profound?

(Enter the Doctor)

Doctor Goodly Pure:

'Tis I, Doctor Goodly Pure.
What seems to be the matter here?
I see a wounded man I fear.
I see a wounded man, for sure.

Father Christmas:

This good man in fight was stabbed.
It seems to be within his abs.
Have you treated such a case as this?

I fear he has no breath, no hiss.

Doctor:

My cures are many.
My treatments are plenty.
Bleeding wounds are my passion.
I treat them all in my good fashion.

Ole Bessie:

Sir, what might thy good fashion be,
Frock tail coat and knickers tight?
Seems odd to treat one in a fight,
With such a fashion code for thee.

Doctor:

No fashion code, no pun intended,
A play on words 'tis all it is.
Please do not be at all offended,
For I come to be a friend of his,
And treat his wounds with skill and measure,
Knowing that my skills give pleasure.

Old Bessie:

What pleasure skills give you this man,
So close to death where he did land?
 If you come in jest, quick, out the door,
And we will see you never more.

Doctor:

Good lady do not judge in haste.
My pleasure is the cure of life.
I'll give this man an herb to taste,
To give him strength. Go find his wife.

(Here the doctor gives Freddy a drink of an herb.
Freddy has a spasm and, gasping for air, sits up looking
wildly at the audience. Father Christmas leaves to find
Freddy's wife.)

Freddy, the Kindly Fool:

Am I dreaming, dead, or living,
Sitting here upon this floor?
Good people see that I am giving,
Breath to life for evermore.

(In rushes Lady May, Freddy's wife, with Father
Christmas.)

Lady May:

Husband! Husband! 'Tis I Lady May.
Good Father Christmas came this evening,
To say my Freddy is alive and breathing,
The breath of life this Christmas day.

(Freddy stands up.)

Freddy the Kindly Fool:

Blessings to you my Lady May,
And blessings to Doctor Goodly Pure.
What is your fee on this great day,
For restoring breath with your fine cure?

Doctor:

I have studied in many lands,
To find the cures I have at hand,
For treating all conditions,
With native customs and traditions.
My fees therefore are quite unique,
And fit the illness that I treat.

Lady May:

For bringing Freddy back to life,
How does one choose the proper fee?
Neither rich nor poor are we,
And living can present such strife.

Father Christmas:

Christmas time is here to offer,
The act of giving, to fill the coffers,
For this service to Freddy and Lady May.
We ask our friends to show the way,
To give Doctor Goodly Pure his rightful pay,

On this bright and glorious Christmas Day.

(In rush 10 actors from the community theatre troupe and proceed to fill the coffers with fake bills to pay Doctor Goodly Pure.)

Father Christmas:

Blessings to all this Christmas Day.
We hope that you enjoyed our play?
Be on your way and have good reason,
To know the meaning of the season.

The festival was well attended and a joy for all who participated in the day's events. With all of the activities going on, six PM. came about rather quickly, or so it seemed. An old fashion town crier roamed through the crowd at five forty announcing that everyone should begin taking their place in the performance tent to receive information regarding the evening's performances. People poured into the performance tent. Taking their seats, Mr. Summers came forward to make announcements.

"Good evening to all. I trust this has been a special day of fun and frolic for everyone? However, there is more entertainment yet to come. At this time, I want to thank all of our performers and vendors for their contribution making this festival such a success. I also extend a special thank you to our staff in the Tack Room Gift Shop and Horseshoe Cafe for their presence and patience, fulfilling our visitor's needs and supporting the Benbuerger Museum on a daily basis. You are very special to all of us. Lastly, I want to thank all of the staff at the Benbuerger Museum for their tireless work and effort to make every day a special day at the museum. This gift of the Twelfth Night Festival would never exist without their dedication and expertise. For this evening's entertainment, the museum will open at six thirty for visitors to enter and gather around the entrance hall. The festivities will begin at seven-thirty. Seating is on a first come, first served basis, but seating will be available for everyone. The entertainment this evening is of a more formal nature beginning with our traditional Christmas pops concert, provided by the Allegro Instrumental Ensemble from Champion Community College. Consisting of strings, woodwinds, brass, and percussion, this outstanding group has won many awards in the music field; we look forward to their performance. In addition, the modern dance troupe, The Adepts, will be performing some special dances with modern interpretation. Once again, the choir from St. Francis Academy will sing a variety of songs to enliven our festival theme."

"We have a very special treat for you this evening, as we introduce two of our museum employees, D.J. Cuddles and Lily Bejon, performing a Segway ballet. This idea came about upon seeing a gentleman enter the museum on a Segway PT unit and proceed to explore the first floor. Being very creative, both D.J. and Lily wanted to see just what could be done with Segway movements. Thus, a Segway ballet was born. After weeks of training on the Segway plus hours spent on choreography, costumes, and music, their Segway ballet will be a unique experience for all of us."

"But first, we have another ceremony to fulfill. That is choosing the King and Queen of the Twelfth Night Festival. This custom has to do with a special cake called by several names: Twelfth Night Cake, Plumb Cake, and King Cake. Contained within the cake are a dried bean and a dried pea. The male who eats the piece of cake with the bean becomes the King, and the female who eats the piece of cake with the pea becomes the Queen. Our pastry chef, Edward, from the Horseshoe Cafe, has prepared such a cake. The cake has been divided into small sections for the male and female actors from Champion Community College to choose. At this time, will the males enter stage left and the females enter stage right."

As the group assembled, Edward and three servers from the cafe came to the front of the stage beside Mr. Summers. There were four trays of cake already cut to choose from, two trays for the females and two trays for the males. Upon a signal from Mr. Summers,
Edward and his server passed out the cake to the males. The other two servers passed out cake to the females. Within a matter of minutes, a King and Queen came forward to the center of the stage. With a trumpet fanfare from the Allegro Instrumental Ensemble, Edward crowned King James, and Mr. Summers crowned Queen Julia. A cape was placed around the shoulders of each royal recipient.

"This ends our daytime ceremony," stated Mr. Summers. "Shortly the newly crowned King and Queen of the Twelfth Night Festival will lead all of you to the museum for this evening's performances."

With another trumpet fanfare, the brass ensemble lead King James and Queen Julia through the visitors in the performance tent. The visitors followed to the museum for all to take a seat. As the procession made their way to the museum, everyone noticed the changing weather pattern, as the cold front moved in bringing quite a chill to the daytime's warm moist air. Also, clouds were gathering in the sky. Cell phones came to attention as people checked weather reports. Could be quite an interesting evening . . . weather-wise!

As the crowd filed into the entrance hall of the museum, the King and Queen each took their seat on thrones atop a platform to the left of the music room, leaving enough space for Lily to move forward on her Segway. Promptly at seven-thirty, the pops concert began with a variety of music including show tunes, music with Christmas themes, marches, and waltzes. During the concert, the choir joined in singing several selections including special music they prepared for the evening. The dance troupe performed several of the show tune sequences and included some special routines of their own. It was a fun, exciting evening for all to enjoy.

While all of this was going on, Lily and D.J. were busy going over last minute details of their segway ballet sequence via radio communication.

"Lily, come back," requested D.J.

"Go for Lily."

"Lily. What's your 20?"

"I'm here D.J., in the morning room," shouted Lily. "I'm so nervous I could just pee in my pants. Where are you?"

"I'm in the library," said D.J. "Hang in there Lily. Everything is going to be fine. I have checked my Segway and tested it out in all the choreographed movements. Have you checked your Segway?"

"Yes," acknowledged Lily. "Everything works fine. I still worry if my skirt will get caught in the wheels. I shortened the length a little just to be sure. I can't believe we are next. Oh, Lord, why did we decide to do this anyway? What a crazy idea."

"It's a brilliant idea." said D.J. "We have practiced so long to get everything just right. It will be a spectacular performance for all to enjoy,"

"I certainly hope you are right," added Lily. "I will be fine when we get out there and make the first move. This waiting drives me insane!"

"Remember, Lily. Take a deep breath and repeat our mantra: serenity now, serenity now. Are you doing it?" asked D.J.

"Oh, that's what you tell Simone to say to bring her back into focus!" exclaimed Lily.

"It works for everybody," said D.J. "Take a deep breath and repeat: serenity now, serenity now."

"What are you trying to do, hypnotize me? It's not working!" yelled Lily.

"Well, stand on your head and get some blood up to your brain," said D.J., laughing out loud.

"You are just impossible," yelled Lily.

"I know," soothed D.J. "That's why you love me. Mr. Summers will give us a 'heads up' when we need to take our places. Remember: serenity now, serenity now!'"

With an over and out, D.J. and Lily waited for their cue to come forward in front of the music room.

It would soon be time for Lily and me to come forward to perform. I was just as nervous as Lily, but I would never let it be known, because I would never hear the end of it. Mr. Summers stepped forward to the opening of the music room to make the announcement about our performance.

"We have a special treat for you this evening," stated Mr. Summers. "For those of you who were not present in the performance tent earlier, we have two employees, Lily Bejon and D.J. Cuddles, who will be performing a special ballet on a Segway transportation device. This idea came about when they observed a visitor to our museum touring the first floor on a Segway. Lily and D.J. were fascinated by the various Segway movements the gentleman performed. This event opened their creative minds, and a ballet was born. We offer a special thank you to Annabelle Morrison, choreographer from The Adepts modern dance troupe, for her expertise in staging this ballet. We also thank Mr. Rodney Pimm for the many hours of training for Lily and D.J. to learn the various movements of the Segway. Because of this introduction to the Segway, Benburger Museum is working closely with Ziggy Albright of Albright Human Transport Systems, Inc. to establish a future outdoor Segway tour at the museum. You will be receiving information about this tour at a later date. Now, let us sit back and enjoy this special Segway ballet."

Lily and I came out from the library and morning room to meet at the entrance of the music room. From there we turned, coming forward down to the center of the entrance hall. Then we made a half turn, and faced one another. "Break a leg," I whispered. Lily rolled her eyes and smiled.

As the applause died down, we waited for our CD music to begin. It seemed like we waited an eternity until the first musical note of the introduction began. We were just at the point of the first ballet movement, when there was a loud crash from outside the museum. The whole house shook and everyone became quiet. Our music stopped, and Lily and I waited in anticipation of what the next installment of this strange event might bring. It seemed like the cold front met the warm front, and Nature Mom married them with a loud crash of thunder. "Thanks Mom, for adding your own special percussion rhythm to our ballet," I thought. "What's next?"

Never ask, "What's next!" That's the kind of cue Mr. Murphy likes. You can just visualize him salivating, rubbing his hands together, and smiling with glee, waiting to strike at the most inopportune time.

Lily turned white and cried, "I just knew something was going to happen. You know how psychic I am."

"It will be fine," I said, with as much determination and positive attitude I could muster.

With that thought to ease my mind, there was another crash of thunder and the power went out. "Hey," Murph. "You and Nature Mom got something going on? Be kind you two."

A loud cry exploded from the audience, and then, all was quiet, except for the occasional hushed small talk from around the room. The darkness took on an eerie quality lit by some glowing candles and fireplaces from the surrounding rooms. Everyone waited to see what would happen next. Then, from the music room, a small light was noticed. A loan flute player sounded the beginning notes of the beautiful *Behold a Star from Jacob Shining*, from the oratory, <u>Christus,</u> written by Felix Bartholdy Mendelssohn. As the flute played, small headband LED lights began to lighten the music room as the instrumentalist and choir lit them to see their music. They always had them, not knowing under what conditions they might have to perform. Slowly, other lights appeared as hosts and security personnel came forward with their flashlight-work light combination units with 37 LED lights each unit. Some lights were pointed up onto the walls and others were pointed toward the floor of the entrance hall. Three security personnel came forward with powerful battery pack halogen spot lights. All three lights were placed on the floor of the entrance hall facing the music room. A runway of light joined the beautiful star-filled room that created a feeling of expectation. Then, as on cue, the St. Francis Academy began to sing as the Allegro Instrumental Ensemble played the beautiful Mendelssohn score. Spurred by a force of action, grace, and beauty, The Adept dance troupe came forward out of the library surrounding Lily and D.J. Annabelle whispered, "You know all the Segway movements. Join us and flow with the music. Remember, free spirits always follow the rhythm of life."

This was certainly not the music that Lily and D.J. had practiced to perform, but they too began to move by the influence of the instrumental ensemble, singers, and dancers. They guided their Segways with incredible synchronous movements that flowed effortlessly becoming one with the ensemble. The audience was spellbound, and not a sound was heard anywhere. Even Nature Mom and Murph were quiet.

At the end of the performance no one moved. The combined performance of music, dance, singing, and the ballet offered such a combined melding of beauty and joy, it was hard to find ways to express the many emotions that everyone felt. Some were joyfully wiping tears from their eyes. Others pondered the experience and were assessing their feelings, and how to express them.

Finally, there was another explosion, as the audience stood up and burst into applause. The performing Adept dance troupe, including Lily and D.J., already in the entrance hall, took their bows. Parting in the middle, the St. Francis Academy choir, and the Allegro Instrumental Ensemble came forward for their bows. After several group bows, the performers filed back into the music room.

The audience began to quiet down as Mr. Summers appeared at the entrance door of the museum. He thanked everyone for being part of such a memorable Twelfth Night Festival. He further thanked King James and Queen Julia for their royal presence residing over the evening's performances. Further announcements confirmed that shuttle service would be available until all guests were safely transported to their cars to drive home and tour groups boarded their buses. Hosts and security guards quickly came forward with their LED pen-work lights and halogen spotlights to help usher the guests safely out of the museum. When the front doors were opened, a light fluffy snow was falling leading everyone out into a new world of calm beauty.

Happenings

This Twelfth Night Festival was talked about for weeks and was never really forgotten. The afternoon of January fifth began with a jovial, enthusiastic crowd. Visitors enjoyed the variety of selections the vendors' offered. The outdoor entertainment was well received, with the unicyclist weaving through the crowd, followed by clowns, jesters, and bands of mummers wielding their wooden swords to pick a fight. Children loved the face painting and hair tinting. The indoor performance tent was always full. Everyone enjoyed the variety of plays, music, and slap stick comedy. The addition of the mummers play was a great success. A new play would definitely be offered next year.

As the day progressed and evening approached, visitors looked forward to the pops concert by the Allegro Instrumental Ensemble. The addition of The Adepts modern dance troupe was a new event this year and well received. The vocal music by the St. Francis Academy always created a festive atmosphere. However, the most anticipated event for all to witness was the Segway ballet by Lily and D.J. Nothing like this had ever been performed before.

The interesting events that took place between Nature Mom and Murph were questioned by all beginning with loud noises and ending with soft, white snow. Various modes of rationalization to understand this chain of events were tossed around like leaves scattered about in a wind storm. Some said, "How odd." Others said, "It must have been fate." A group of older women said, "Well I never saw anything like that!" Still others had no spoken comments, but everyone was truly affected by the combined unexpected evening performances: the music, the dance, the voices, the Segway ballet, and the interesting weather changes. For many, this Christmas became a very special one to remember.

Lily and I, along with all of the performers including King James and Queen Julia, gathered together in the entrance hall after the visitors had left. Many hosts and security guards joined us. With the usual kudos of outstanding performance, brilliant dance routines, and lovely music, everyone was still trying to comprehend the total impact of the unexpected performance. The Mendelssohn score, *Behold a Star from Jacob Shining*, was to be performed at the end of Lily and D.J.'s ballet to close the Christmas season at Benburger Museum and introduce the season of Epiphany. Somehow the power outage, with the interesting lighting by the choir, instrumental group, hosts, and security personnel, created an atmosphere of expectation. When the flute began playing the introduction to the piece, and the choir began to sing, the dancers became motivated. Coming forward, the dancers surrounded Lily and DJ, suggesting for all to improvise movement *as* free spirits expressing their individuality to the rhythm of life.

As everyone left the museum to go to their cars and buses to return home, Lily and D.J. took a minute to reflect on the evening's unexpected performance.

"This was the most amazing experience of my life," said Lily.

"I agree with that," added D.J. "Never in my wildest imagination could I have expected such a performance. It's going to take some time for me to process everything and fully understand just what happened."

"Is it really necessary to understand what happened?" said Lily? "Sometimes it is better to let an experience happen and not process it so much. I think we all become too mind full at times trying to rationalize experiences rather than being just mindful of the event. Being mindful allows the expression to unfold within, creating a new image of inner knowing and understanding."

"Hmm," said D.J. "I'll have to think about that."

"Don't think," said Lily. "Just allow".

"Will do," said D.J. "Have a safe drive home. I'll give you a call tomorrow. Love ya."

"Back at you," said Lily. "Drive carefully."

Even the drive home was magical with the snow lightly falling. It was hard not to think about the events of the evening. There was little traffic on the roads because of the snow. D.J. was glad, as it was hard to keep completely focused on driving. At long last, 3782 Willow Ridge Drive came into view. Turning into the driveway and pushing the garage door opener, D.J. drove into the garage. Shutting the car motor off, getting out of the car, he walked into the mudroom area leading into the kitchen. Swanson was right there to greet him, expressing a multitude of cat meows, purrs, and much head rubbing. D.J. picked him up and gave him a long hug while rubbing his head.

"Hey," buddy. "Did you get your dinner? Let's go check," said D.J.

After food, water, and litter box check, D.J. fixed a cup of coffee for himself, grabbed a snack, and relaxed a moment with Swanson sitting in his lap. After some light conversation leading to some yawns of exhaustion, Swanson and D.J. headed for the bedroom. Swanson claimed his spot on the bed and proceeded to clean his face, paws, and other cat parts. At the same time, D.J. prepared himself for a much needed night's rest. After climbing into bed, Swanson snuggled up beside him. Turning off the light, D.J. faced Swanson and said, "Boy, do I have a story to tell you!"

Contemplation

Swanson was thrilled to learn of the events that took place in the museum during Twelfth Night. He was totally fascinated about the unexpected performance. In fact, he became so excited over the dual conspiracy of Nature Mom and Murph, he had a hairball attack! "That's OK," I said. "I understand completely. When the lights went out just before our performance, I almost had a panic attack,"

Twelfth Night was over, and the winter season was upon us. For the months of January and February, visitor count dropped at the museum, mainly because of weather and children in school. Family vacations were over, so this gave the housekeeping department some much needed time to start major cleaning projects in the museum. Some part-time employees were put on their usual winter layoff, to be called back on an "as needed" basis, through the middle of March. Full schedules resumed April 1st making preparations for the English Garden Festival including a formal flower display. Lily and I were on the layoff list. With the weeks of preparation for our Segway ballet, both of us were dead to drop. It was hibernation time!

I never really forgot the experience of the unexpected performance. It was hard not to think about the events that took place in the museum during the evening of December 5th. I knew the circumstances that lead up to the unexpected performance, and how it came about. The thoughts that kept running through my mind were not how the Segway moved or how the costumes looked. My thoughts were more directed as to why this happened? What was the message learned from this experience? I thought a lot about what Lily said, about not being mind full, but being mindful of any happening and let it unfold. I realized that at times we do load our mind with all kinds of data trying to resolve a situation. If we just stepped back and became mindful of the situation, a new insight of understanding would evolve.

I did try to calm my mind and step back to allow the meaning of our unexpected performance to unfold. As the days passed, I came to understand we have many unexpected performances in life. Each one gives us a wakeup call. It shakes us out of our sedentary ways and moves us forward. It often gives us the insight to follow a dream; perhaps to go back to school to finish that degree started years ago; to begin a new vocation that you have always wished to peruse; or to enjoy the knowing that all is well. There is one thing for sure. All unexpected performances create change, allowing us to make new choices to enrich our lives, leading us in a new direction or complementing where we are as life unfolds before us.

Thanks to Nature Mom and Murph, some of life's qualities of being were brought to mind. The electrical power failed during our performance at Benburger

Museum, but *light* still prevailed in the semi-darkness. The *power of love* called all performers to create a mass energy that expressed itself as *beauty*. Through beauty, everyone experienced *joy*.

At 3782 Willow Ridge Drive, Swanson and I settled down to enjoy the winter. I slept, ate, read, and watched TV. Swanson slept, ate, talked, and watched TV. Our conversations continued on a daily basis, and we took our walks, weather permitting. Swanson had to show off the new sweater he got for Christmas. I enjoyed my new winter coat and boots. Life was good, and we were at peace. So, life goes on. And so it is.

About the Author:

Robert hails from Charlotte, North Carolina. With a BA degree in Education from the University of North Carolina., Robert taught junior high school for three years before enlisting in the US Army. Several years later, Robert received a Doctor of Chiropractic degree from Cleveland Chiropractic College in Kansas City, Missouri. After a thirty year practice in the Kansas City area, Robert moved to Whidbey Island, Washington, to continue study in the techniques of Therapeutic Massage and Structural Muscular Balancing. Robert moved to Western North Carolina in 2007 where he currently lives and works in the hospitality and health fields.

Being told several times throughout his life that he would become a writer, Robert put this idea behind him until he met a co-worker who sparked his interest in writing. Unexpected Performance is Roberts's first book, and contains both true and imagined happenings based upon his experiences in the field of hospitality.

Robert is also a contributor to the online humor magazine, Humoroutcasts.com